The Cello of Mr. O

by JANE CUTLER · illustrated by GREG COUCH

DUTTON CHILDREN'S BOOKS · NEW YORK

Library of Congress Cataloging-in-Publication Data
Cutler, Jane.
The Cello of Mr. O / by Jane Cutler; illustrated by Greg Couch.—1st ed. p. cm.
Summary: When a concert cellist plays in the square for his neighbors
in a war-besieged city, his priceless instrument is destroyed by a mortar shell,
but he finds the courage to return the next day to perform with a harmonica.
ISBN 0-525-46119-1 (hc)
[1. Violoncello—Fiction. 2. War—Fiction. 3. Courage—Fiction.
4. Musicians—Fiction.] I. Couch, Greg, ill. II. Title.
PZ7.C985Ce 1999
[E]—dc21 98-42692 CIP AC

Published in the United States 1999 by Dutton Children's Books,
a division of Penguin Young Readers Group
345 Hudson Street, New York, New York 10014
www.penguin.com
Designed by Ellen M. Lucaire
Manufactured in China   First Edition
7 9 10 8 6

For Birgitta
—J.C.

To Robin, with love
—G.C.

Here we are, surrounded and under attack.

My father and most of the other fathers, the older brothers—even some of the grandfathers—have gone to fight. So we stay, children and women, the old and the sick, managing as best we can.

I am afraid almost all the time.

At night, from my window, I can see the white trails of tracer fire and the orange flash of mortars in the sky. I pretend I am watching shooting stars and meteors.

The streets of our city are littered with bricks, dust, and broken glass. We have no heating oil. Last winter, we slept in our clothes in the kitchen, next to a sheet-metal stove Papa put together before he left.

We used up all our wood. If something doesn't change by the time winter comes again, we will have to burn furniture and books to keep warm.

Food is scarce, of course. And water. We collect rainwater in bowls and buckets. And we go to distribution centers and bring water home.

Some people carry their heavy containers of water in shopping carts,

some in wheelbarrows. In winter, many of us use sleds. Last week, Mama and I saw a woman hauling water in a wheelchair.

Each Wednesday at four, the relief truck comes to a street right outside our square. We wait in line to receive soap, cooking oil, canned fish, flour.

Nothing is as it was: shops, cars, and apartments have been destroyed. Schools are closed, the electricity is usually out, and there is no gas at all. Even the telephones don't work.

Many people have left.

Some, like Mama's friend Marya, stay because they have no place else to go. And some, like my mother, have decided to stay—no matter what.

Mama can't stand the idea of Papa coming back to nothing. She wants us to be here.

Mama sighs. "This is not the first time in history that such a thing has happened," she tells me.

It may not be the first time it has happened. But it is the first time it has happened to me.

I am angry almost all the time.

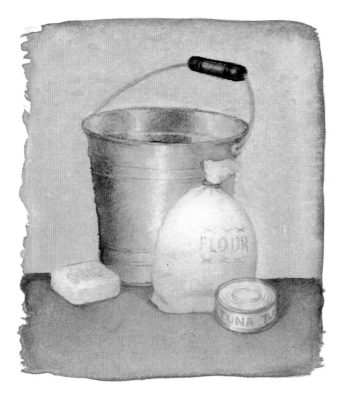

My friends and I stay close to home, usually inside our large apartment building, sitting under the stairs. We pass the time playing cards and word games. Reading books. Drawing. Talking. We imagine what we would have if we could eat whatever we wanted.

Sometimes we can't sit still a minute longer, and we run through the halls, laughing and making noise.

Then Mr. O flings open his door. "Quiet, you kids!" he shouts. As if kids were a bad thing.

When the relief truck comes at four o'clock on Wednesdays, everyone goes into the street. It feels like a party, being outside with so many other people for a change.

Even Mr. O stands in line.

But he doesn't chat. He just waits, looking away from the rest of us.

"A thinker," my mother says quietly, nodding in his direction.
"A thinker," her friend Marya says, but in a mocking tone.
Marya doesn't agree with my mother. Neither do I.
Mr. O isn't thinking. He is just being unfriendly.

We children don't like Mr. O. Whenever one of us can find a paper bag, we blow it up with air and then pop it right outside his apartment door. It sounds just like a shell exploding!

We laugh and run, imagining his fear.

When he is not waiting in line for supplies with the rest of us, Mr. O plays his cello.

It is a fine cello, one of the best. My father, who loves music, too—who plays tender songs and lively tunes on the harmonica—told me this about the cello of Mr. O.

"The front and the back of that excellent cello were carved out of German fiddleback maple and hand-rubbed with a special polish made in France," said my father.

"The neck of the cello was made of mahogany from Honduras, and the fingerboard of ebony, probably from Ceylon," he said.

"As for the bow," my father continued, "it was carved out of a soft wood that grows in Brazil. The ivory on its tip came from Africa."

"People all over the world had to cooperate to make the cello of Mr. O," my father said.

My father told me about Mr. O, too. "When he was young, he traveled around the world, playing his cello in great halls for hundreds of people who cheered when he finished, and threw flowers."

If my father knew about the paper bags, he would be angry.

But Papa is far away, fighting somewhere in the mountains. He has taken his harmonica and all his warm clothes with him, and we have no idea when we will see him again.

It is four o'clock in the afternoon, a dull fall Wednesday. My friend Elena and I are playing jacks under the stairs. We hear the supply truck roar up. But we are lazy, and for once, we don't rush outside to wait with the others.

We hear the footsteps of people leaving their apartments, leaving the building.

We hear the murmur of talk and laughter.

Then we hear the rocket hit.

The truck is destroyed. Some people we know are badly hurt.

Now, even though we clear away the rubble and smooth over the ground, supplies will not be brought here. We are too easy a target, they

tell us. Now we will have to walk for miles to get anything, and nothing will happen to make even one day a week better than the others.

But on the first Wednesday after the rocket, at exactly four o'clock, Mr. O appears, all dressed up, carrying his cello, carrying a chair.

He marches out into the middle of the square, where everyone can see him.

He sets up his chair.

He takes out his cello.

He tightens his horsehair bow and rubs it with rosin.

Then he takes a deep breath.

He plays.

"The music of Bach," Mama tells me, her face shining, as we listen to the complicated music, the powerful and reassuring notes.

How he plays, our Mr. O! As if he were on the stage of a grand, warm hall, playing for people who will throw flowers. As if he were not alone in the center of a deserted square in a besieged city, where even a relief truck will no longer come.

"They will kill him!" Marya cries fearfully.

"They would not bother to kill an old man playing a cello," Mama says.

I am not so sure.

Because the music of the cello makes us feel less angry. And the courage of the cellist makes us less afraid.

If they guess, it could be reason enough for them to want to stop the music, which feeds us as truly as the supplies brought by the truck did.

Mr. O does not play only on Wednesdays. Every day at four o'clock, he and his cello appear.

One day, after he has started playing, Mr. O gets a cramp in his leg.
He leans the cello against his chair and hobbles about, shaking his leg.
We hear a fusillade of exploding shells.
We see clouds of black smoke.

Finally, when the smoke clears, we see that the cellist is unharmed.
But all that remains of the cello is splintered wood and tangled strings.
What will feed us now? I wonder.

It is the very next day that I find the brown paper bag. It is a small one, and crumpled. I smooth it out as best I can. Then I put it under Papa's heavy dictionary and leave it there all night.

In the morning, I choose the best crayons I have from the cigar box where I keep them. Most of them are now just stubs of crayons. Still, I have many different colors left.

Carefully, on the crinkly paper bag, I draw. I draw a picture of Mr. O in his dark suit sitting on a chair, playing a cello. Then I draw bright flowers falling all around him.

When I finish, I take the picture and tiptoe up to Mr. O's apartment. I press my ear against the door and listen. Silence. Carefully, quietly, I slip the picture underneath the door. And then I run.

To everyone's surprise, promptly at four o'clock that afternoon, out of the building comes Mr. O, carrying a chair.

He sees me at my window, and he bows to me and smiles.

Then, from the pocket of his coat, he draws a small, shiny object. A harmonica!

From then on, for one hour every single day, Mr. O sits in the square and plays his harmonica.

The melodies sound sad and sweet and small, and very different from the grand songs Mr. O played on his cello.

"It is Bach, nevertheless," Mama says.

The music makes us feel happy.

And the courage of the harmonica player makes us less afraid.